W9-AVF-939

Too Many Books!

Too Many Books!

BY CAROLINE FELLER BAUER

ILLUSTRATED BY DIANE PATERSON

PUFFIN BOOKS

PUFFIN BOOKS

Viking Penguin Inc., 40 West 23rd Street, New York, New York 10010, U.S.A.
Penguin Books Ltd, Harmondsworth, Middlesex, England
Penguin Books Australia Ltd, Ringwood, Victoria, Australia
Penguin Books Canada Limited, 2801 John Street, Markham, Ontario, Canada L3R 1B4
Penguin Books (N.Z.) Ltd, 182–190 Wairau Road, Auckland 10, New Zealand

First published by Frederick Warne & Co., Inc., 1984
Published in Picture Puffins 1986
Text copyright © Caroline Felier Bauer, 1984
Illustrations copyright © Diane Paterson, 1984
All rights reserved
Printed in U.S.A. by Rae Publishing Co., Cedar Grove, New Jersey
Set in Aster

Library of Congress Cataloging in Publication Data
Bauer, Caroline Feller.   Too many books!
Summary: Maralou's idea to reduce her enormous book collection benefits many people.
[1. Books and reading—Fiction] I. Paterson, Diane, 1946– ill. II. Title.
PZ7.B3258To 1986   [E]   86-4877   ISBN 0-14-050632-2

Except in the United States of America, this book is sold subject to the condition
that it shall not, by way of trade or otherwise, be lent, re-sold, hired out, or
otherwise circulated without the publisher's prior consent in any form of binding
or cover other than that in which it is published and without a similar condition
including this condition being imposed on the subsequent purchaser.

For Ann Symons, who always returns a borrowed book   —C.F.B.

Maralou loved books, even as a baby.

When Maralou learned to read, she read all of the time.
She read at the breakfast table.
She read on the bus to school.
She read in the bathtub.
She read while she jumped rope

. . . or tried to.

Every week, Maralou took her wagon to the library to borrow books.
The following week, Maralou brought the books back and borrowed more.

One day during Book Week,
Maralou's Aunt Molly *gave*
her a book. Fantastic!
Now that she owned her
own book, she could read it
over and over again.

Maralou wanted more books. She asked for books whenever someone wanted to give her a present.
    She was given books for her birthday,
    For Halloween,

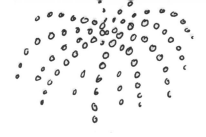

. . . and even for the Fourth of July.

Maralou also earned money so she could buy books.
    She cat sat.
    She sold lemonade.
    She had a garage sale.
    She tried to sell her little brother

        . . . but that didn't work.

After a while, Maralou had a lot of books.
Mom and Dad built shelves for the books
but there still wasn't enough room.
There were books in the bathtub,
on every table,
all over the floor,   . . . and even in the refrigerator.

Maralou had too many books! Mom couldn't get out the front door.

Dad couldn't get in the back door.

But Maralou still loved books and wanted more to read.
How could she make room?

Then Maralou had an idea. Maybe other people would
love books too! So she decided to give some books away.
    She gave a book to a little boy on his way to school.
    She gave a book to the mail carrier.
    She left books at the doctor's office

                    . . . and at the playground.

Soon the whole town was reading all the time.

People bought books, borrowed books, and traded books.
The town was bulging with books.

The mayor called the librarian in the next town
to see if they would like to have some books.

They did, and it wasn't long before *all* the nearby towns were borrowing

READ!

l trading and reading and sharing books.

But Maralou didn't notice.
She sat in front of the library

. . . reading a book.